TEAM SPIRIT®
SMART BOOKS FOR YOUNG FANS

THE CHICAGO WHITE SOX

BY
MARK STEWART

New Hanover County Public Library
201 Chestnut Street
Wilmington, North Carolina 28401

NORWOODHOUSE PRESS
CHICAGO, ILLINOIS

Norwood House Press
P.O. Box 316598
Chicago, Illinois 60631

For information regarding Norwood House Press, please visit our website at:
www.norwoodhousepress.com or call 866-565-2900.

All photos courtesy of Getty Images except the following:
Tom DiPace (4, 8, 14), Author's Collection (6, 16, 17, 18, 26, 28, 33, 37, 43 bottom right),
SportsChrome (10), Topps, Inc. (15, 23, 24, 27, 29, 34 bottom right, 36, 42 bottom), Sweet Caporal (20),
John Morrell & Co. (21), Black Book Partners Archives (22, 35 top, 41, 43 left, 45),
F.W. Rueckheim & Brother (34 bottom left), Exhibit Supply Co. (34 top, 40),
Associated Press (35 bottom left), Cleveland Indians (38), Wilson Franks (39),
Pacific Trading Cards (42 top), The Sporting News (43 top), Matt Richman (48).
Cover Photo: Associated Press

The memorabilia and artifacts pictured in this book are presented for educational and informational purposes,
and come from the collection of the author.

Editor: Mike Kennedy
Designer: Ron Jaffe
Project Management: Black Book Partners, LLC.
Special thanks to Topps, Inc.

Library of Congress Cataloging-in-Publication Data

Stewart, Mark, 1960-
  The Chicago White Sox / by Mark Stewart. -- Libary ed.
     p. cm. -- (Team spirit)
  Includes bibliographical references and index.
  Summary: "A Team Spirit Baseball edition featuring the Chicago White Sox
that chronicles the history and accomplishments of the team. Includes access
to the Team Spirit website, which provides additional information, updates
and photos"--Provided by publisher.
  ISBN 978-1-59953-477-0 (library : alk. paper) -- ISBN 978-1-60357-357-3
(ebook) 1. Chicago White Sox (Baseball team)--History--Juvenile
literature. I. Title.
  GV875.C58S83 2012
  796.357'640977311--dc23
                                              2011048487

Manufactured in the United States of America in North Mankato, Minnesota.
196N—012012

COVER PHOTO: The White Sox celebrate their 2005 championship.

TABLE OF CONTENTS

CHAPTER	PAGE
MEET THE WHITE SOX	4
GLORY DAYS	6
HOME TURF	12
DRESSED FOR SUCCESS	14
WE WON!	16
GO-TO GUYS	20
CALLING THE SHOTS	24
ONE GREAT DAY	26
LEGEND HAS IT	28
IT REALLY HAPPENED	30
TEAM SPIRIT	32
TIMELINE	34
FUN FACTS	36
TALKING BASEBALL	38
GREAT DEBATES	40
FOR THE RECORD	42
PINPOINTS	44
GLOSSARY	46
EXTRA INNINGS	47
INDEX	48

ABOUT OUR GLOSSARY

In this book, there may be several words that you are reading for the first time. Some are sports words, some are new vocabulary words, and some are familiar words that are used in an unusual way. All of these words are defined on page 46. Throughout the book, sports words appear in **bold type**. Regular vocabulary words appear in ***bold italic type***.

MEET THE WHITE SOX

Baseball is part of the rhythm of life in Chicago, Illinois. It has been that way for nearly 150 years. The White Sox have been an important part of that *tradition* since the start of the 20th century. They have competed with the Cubs for the hearts of Chicago baseball fans for more than 100 years.

Both teams have provided Chicago with wonderful memories and thrills. But it was the White Sox that gave the city something it hadn't had in more than 80 years: a **World Series** championship.

This book tells the story of the White Sox. Their fans like players who are ready to roll up their sleeves and work hard to win. That is the spirit of Chicago, and it's what makes people smile whenever the White Sox win.

Paul Konerko leads the team off the field after a 2011 victory. He is one of the many White Sox who have captured the spirit of Chicago baseball.

GLORY DAYS

What could be better than having a baseball team playing in your town? In 1901, Chicago fans learned the answer: having two teams. That year, the **American League (AL)** played its first season. The AL's best team was the Chicago White Stockings.

Almost from the start, newspapers shortened the team's name to White Sox. That's what it has been ever since.

The White Sox were owned by Charles Comiskey. He had been a star player in the 1880s. In the 1890s, he bought a team in the **minor leagues**. Comiskey decided to move this club to Chicago and join the AL. The city's **National League (NL)** team—now known as the Cubs—played on the north side of town. The White Sox played on the south side. This is still true today.

The White Sox had some of baseball's greatest players in the early years of the 20th century. Their stars included George Davis,

Nick Altrock, Ed Walsh, Eddie Cicotte, Ray Schalk, Eddie Collins, Happy Felsch, Buck Weaver, and Joe Jackson.

The White Sox won the World Series in 1906 under the guidance of **player-manager** Fielder Jones. They won the championship again in 1917. But their best team was the one that captured the **pennant** in 1919. No one could believe it when the White Sox lost the World Series that fall. Later, it was discovered that several members of the team had made bad plays on purpose. These players were thrown out of baseball forever. Many fans still call the 1919 team the "Black Sox."

During the 1920s, 1930s, and 1940s, a handful of stars wore the Chicago uniform, including pitchers Red Faber and Ted Lyons, and hitters Bibb Falk and Luke Appling. But it was not until the 1950s that the White Sox had a team good enough to challenge for the AL pennant again. Led by infielders Nellie Fox and Luis Aparicio, and pitchers Early Wynn and Billy Pierce, the White Sox

finally made it back to the World Series in 1959, but they lost to the Los Angeles Dodgers.

During the 1960s and 1970s, the White Sox continued to find talented pitchers. Joel Horlen, Gary Peters, Tommy John, Wilbur Wood, Jim Kaat, and Goose Gossage were among the best in baseball. The offense was another matter. Players such Pete Ward, Bill Melton, and Dick

Allen were very good hitters, but the Chicago batting order was not *consistent* from one year to the next.

The team's luck did not change in the 1980s or 1990s. During this time, the White Sox managed to put together a powerful attack that included Harold Baines, Carlton Fisk, Robin Ventura, and Frank Thomas. Unfortunately, their pitching failed. Pitchers such as Jack McDowell and Alex Fernandez were excellent during the regular season, but they struggled in the **playoffs**. Chicago reached the **American League Championship Series (ALCS)** in 1983 and 1993, but the team fell short of another pennant both times.

LEFT: Frank Thomas was nicknamed "The Big Hurt" because of how hard he hit the ball.   **ABOVE**: Harold Baines shows off his smooth swing.

In the early years of the 21st century, Chicago fans believed the White Sox were close to returning to the World Series. But their spirits sank when injuries kept Thomas out of the lineup for months at a time. How could Chicago win without its most fearsome hitter? The White Sox found the answer by looking back to the past and focusing on the basics.

Manager Ozzie Guillen helped put together a team that was unbeatable at times. Mark Buehrle was the ace of a great pitching staff that included Jon Garland, Freddy Garcia, Jose Contreras, and Bobby Jenks. The leader on offense was slugging first baseman Paul Konerko. He was joined by Jermaine Dye, Joe Crede, Tadahito Iguchi, A.J. Pierzynski, and Scott Podsednik.

In 2005, the White Sox won the **AL Central** and then raced through the playoffs. They beat the Boston Red Sox in three straight

games. In the ALCS, Chicago lost just once. The White Sox finished their amazing run with a four-game sweep of the Houston Astros in the World Series. The White Sox were champions of baseball for the first time since 1917.

The team continues to learn from the past as it tries to build a winner. The White Sox are at their best when they have strong pitching, good defense, and hitters who come through when the pressure is on. That combination has led to some of baseball's most memorable moments. It is also why fans on the South Side of Chicago can hardly wait for the team's next championship run.

LEFT: Ozzie Guillen holds a meeting on the pitcher's mound.
ABOVE: Mark Buehrle helped Chicago win the 2005 World Series.

The first home for the White Sox was called South Side Park. They played there until 1910, when the team moved to Comiskey Park. That stadium was named after the team's owner, Charles Comiskey. The White Sox stayed there for 81 years.

Today, the team plays in a stadium that many fans call "new Comiskey Park." It opened on April 18, 1991. The stadium is located right across the street from the site of the first Comiskey Park. It has the look and feel of an old-time stadium. The scoreboard erupts with fireworks when the White Sox win an important game. All of the seats in the stadium offer a great view of the field. The new Comiskey includes one feature that was very popular in the old Comiskey—outdoor showers for hot days.

BY THE NUMBERS

- The team's stadium has 41,432 seats.
- The distance from home plate to the left field foul pole is 330 feet.
- The distance from home plate to the center field wall is 400 feet.
- The distance from home plate to the right field foul pole is 335 feet.

Chicago's stadium is alive with energy for a game during the 2007 season.

DRESSED FOR SUCCESS

The White Sox have worn many different uniforms over the years. Most have included *Chicago*, *Sox*, or the letter *C*. The first time *Sox* appeared on the team's uniform was in 1910. But Chicago didn't use all-white socks until 1946.

In 1960, the White Sox were the first team to put names on the backs of their uniforms. In 1967, the team's road uniform spelled out *Chicago White Sox*. This was one of the few times a team has used its city and name together.

During the past 40 years, the White Sox have experimented with some fun ideas. In the 1960s, the team wore powder-blue uniforms on the road. In the 1970s, the White Sox wore red socks for a couple of seasons. In the 1980s, the team tried a modern look, with *Sox* spelled out in big lettering on their caps. Today, the team's home uniforms feature black **pinstripes** and a black cap.

LEFT: Gordon Beckham wears Chicago's 2011 road uniform.
ABOVE: This trading card from the 1960s shows Gary Peters wearing a cap and jersey with *Sox* spelled out in two different styles.

WE WON!

The White Sox won their first pennant in 1901. Chicago relied on strong pitching and daring baserunning to win games. The team's hitters were at their best under pressure. Player-manager Clark Griffith won 24 games on the mound. Fielder Jones led the club with a .311 batting average.

The White Sox won their first World Series in 1906. Their next championship came in 1917. After that, Chicago waited 88 years to capture its third championship. Each time, the White Sox used the same recipe for success.

The 1906 World Series was the only one ever played between Chicago's two teams, the White Sox and Cubs. The Cubs had set a record by winning 116 games during the season. They were expected to win the World Series easily. The White Sox were managed by Fielder Jones, a man who studied

baseball like it was a science. He knew that he had to do something unusual to beat the Cubs.

Twice in this series, Jones handed the ball to a young pitcher named Ed Walsh. Walsh threw a spitball—a pitch that squirted out of his fingers like a watermelon seed, and then moved suddenly as it neared home plate. The Cubs were helpless against Walsh, who won two games and struck out 17 batters. The White Sox split the other four games with the Cubs and won the World Series four games to two.

The White Sox played the New York Giants in the 1917 World Series. Both teams had good hitting and pitching, so it was no surprise when fielding turned out to be the big difference in their games. Chicago fans cheered as their stars—including Joe Jackson, Ray Schalk, and Eddie Collins—made one great defensive play after another. Red Faber and Eddie Cicotte gave the White Sox all the pitching they needed to win four games to two.

RED FABER
PITCHER
CHICAGO "WHITE SOX" A. L.

The White Sox won the AL pennant in 1919 and 1959, but lost in the World Series both times. In 1983, Chicago won the **AL West** and faced the Baltimore Orioles in the ALCS. The White Sox fell in four games. Chicago made it to the playoffs again in 1993 and 2000. Both times the team was unable to win the pennant.

In 2005, the White Sox finally returned to the World Series. Like the great Chicago teams of the past, they had several talented pitchers, including Mark Buehrle, Jon Garland, Freddy Garcia, Jose Contreras, and Bobby

Jenks. They also had very good fielders, including Aaron Rowand, Joe Crede, and Juan Uribe. All year long, the team got important hits from Paul Konerko, Scott Podsednik, and Jermaine Dye.

The White Sox met the Houston Astros in the World Series and played four very close games. Chicago *prevailed* in all of them, including a 14-inning victory in Game 3 and a spine-tingling 1–0 win in Game 4. For the third time in a century, the old formula for success worked once again—pitching plus defense plus timely hitting equaled a championship.

LEFT: Red Faber won three times during the 1917 World Series.
ABOVE: The White Sox celebrate their victory over the Houston Astros.

GO-TO GUYS

To be a true star in baseball, you need more than a quick bat and a strong arm. You have to be a "go-to guy"—someone the manager wants on the pitcher's mound or in the batter's box when it matters most. Fans of the White Sox have had a lot to cheer about over the years, including these great stars …

THE PIONEERS

ED WALSH   Pitcher

- BORN: 5/14/1881 • DIED: 5/26/1959
- PLAYED FOR TEAM: 1904 TO 1916

WALSH, CHICAGO AMER.

Ed Walsh threw a spitball, a tricky pitch that was almost impossible to hit. He won 40 games for the White Sox in 1908 and led the AL in strikeouts twice. The spitball was outlawed in 1920 because it was dangerous to batters.

RAY SCHALK   Catcher

- BORN: 8/12/1892 • DIED: 5/19/1970 • PLAYED FOR TEAM: 1912 TO 1928

In the early 1900s, catchers were expected to stay behind home plate. Ray Schalk used his speed and athletic skills to change the way the position was played. He was a master at fielding bunts and catching pop-ups.

LUKE APPLING   Shortstop

• BORN: 4/2/1907 • DIED: 1/3/1991 • PLAYED FOR TEAM: 1930 TO 1950

Luke Appling was an expert at fouling off tough pitches. He would stay at bat until he earned a walk, or until the pitcher gave him something good to hit. In 1936, Appling led the AL in batting with a .388 average.

BILLY PIERCE   Pitcher

• BORN: 4/2/1927   • PLAYED FOR TEAM: 1949 TO 1961

Billy Pierce was one of the top left-handed pitchers of the 1950s. He was an **All-Star** seven times for the White Sox. Pierce led the AL with a 1.97 **earned run average (ERA)** in 1955 and was a 20-game winner in 1957.

BILLY PIERCE

CHICAGO WHITE SOX

NELLIE FOX   Second Baseman

• BORN: 12/25/1927 • DIED: 12/1/1975
• PLAYED FOR TEAM: 1950 TO 1963

Nellie Fox was a great fielder and baserunner, and he was one of the hardest men in history to strike out. He was the AL's **Most Valuable Player (MVP)** in 1959.

LUIS APARICIO   Shortstop

• BORN: 4/29/1934   • PLAYED FOR TEAM: 1956 TO 1962 & 1968 TO 1970

Luis Aparicio was a superb fielder and daring baserunner. He led the AL in stolen bases in each of his first seven seasons with Chicago.

LEFT: Ed Walsh
ABOVE: Billy Pierce

HAROLD BAINES   Outfielder/Designated Hitter

- BORN: 3/15/1959
- PLAYED FOR TEAM: 1980 TO 1989, 1996 TO 1997 & 2000 TO 2001

Harold Baines was the first player chosen in the 1977 baseball **draft**. He rewarded the White Sox with many great seasons. He became the first Chicago player to hit 20 home runs six years in a row. Baines was at his best when hitting with runners on base.

CARLTON FISK   Catcher

- BORN: 12/26/1947
- PLAYED FOR TEAM: 1981 TO 1993

When Carlton Fisk joined the White Sox at the age of 33, many fans thought he had only a few good seasons left. He led the team to the AL West title in 1983, and then caught for 10 more seasons. Fisk hit more than 200 home runs during his time in Chicago.

OZZIE GUILLEN   Shortstop

- BORN: 1/20/1964   • PLAYED FOR TEAM: 1985 TO 1997

Ozzie Guillen was one of the team's most popular and exciting players. He found ways to win games that did not always show up in his statistics, but no one ever doubted his value. Guillen later managed Chicago to a championship.

FRANK THOMAS — First Baseman/Designated Hitter

- Born: 5/27/1968 • Played for Team: 1990 to 2005

Frank Thomas joined the White Sox in 1990, and it did not take long for him to become the greatest hitter in the team's history. He batted over .300 eight years in a row and was voted the league MVP in 1993 and 1994.

MARK BUEHRLE — Pitcher

- Born: 3/23/1979 • Played for Team: 2000 to 2011

It takes a very special pitcher to throw a **no-hitter**. Mark Buehrle showed how special he was by pitching two of them, in 2007 and 2009. His second was a **perfect game**. No White Sox pitcher had pitched a perfect game since Charlie Robertson in 1922.

PAUL KONERKO — First Baseman

- Born: 3/5/1976
- First Year with Team: 1999

Paul Konerko's sense of humor and knowledge of baseball made him a popular player in Chicago. So did his power hitting. From 2001 to 2011, Konerko belted more than 30 home runs seven times and drove in 100 or more runs six times.

LEFT: Carlton Fisk
RIGHT: Paul Konerko

The White Sox have always believed that good players make good managers. In fact, they have had 11 managers who played their way into the **Hall of Fame.** A twelfth player, Al Lopez, joined them there after his success leading the team. Lopez had

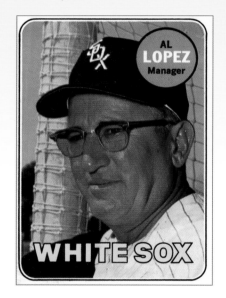

been an All-Star catcher. He understood the importance of good pitching and speed on the basepaths. Lopez led the White Sox to nine winning seasons in a row. In 1959, the team played in the World Series for the first time in 40 years.

One of Chicago's most popular managers was Ozzie Guillen. He was named **Rookie of the Year** with the White Sox in 1985 and played for more than a dozen seasons with the team. Guillen was a daring and talented player. The White Sox thought he would make a good manager and hired him in 2004.

The fans began to wonder if that was a mistake after Guillen made some surprising changes. Chicago had been successful for a

LEFT: Al Lopez
RIGHT: Martians show up at the Chicago dugout in 1959.

long time thanks to its power hitting. Guillen wanted to rely more on pitching and defense. One year later, the White Sox were World Series champions. Guillen managed Chicago for eight seasons in all.

Perhaps the most famous leader of the White Sox was their first owner, Charles Comiskey. He was very strict with his players. At one time he insisted that they wash their own uniforms! From 1901 to 1919, Comiskey's teams won four pennants.

Another famous owner of the White Sox was Bill Veeck. He loved to think up new ways to sell tickets. His first year as owner was 1959. That season the White Sox won the pennant and drew more than a million fans to their games. Many were there the day when Veeck hired a group of "Martians" to kidnap Nellie Fox and Luis Aparicio, his two star players. Fans never knew what to expect from the White Sox with Veeck in charge—and they loved him for it.

ONE GREAT DAY

During the 1950s, the White Sox were known as a team that scored runs one at a time. They played in a big ballpark, so swinging for home runs didn't make much sense. Often they won or lost home games by just one run. It was almost a relief for the players to get out of Chicago and play road games in other stadiums. During the second week of the 1955 season, the White Sox arrived in Kansas City to play the A's.

The A's were not a very good team. In their first eight games, they had already given up 10 or more runs three times. When Bob Nieman belted a homer in the first inning, the White Sox went ahead 4–0. Many of the fans in Municipal Stadium had a feeling it might be a long day. They never imagined just how long it would be.

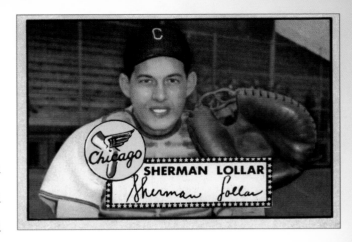

The White Sox scored seven times in the next inning. Sherm Lollar drove in the first run with a home run. He knocked in the seventh run with a single when he came up again. Chicago smashed two more balls into the seats in the third inning to make the score 14–3.

The White Sox weren't done yet. They scored 15 more runs to win 29–6. All told, they hit five doubles and seven home runs. Nieman and Lollar finished with two home runs each. They had 12 **runs batted in (RBIs)** between them. Chicago's pitcher, Jack Harshman, also hit a home run. Minnie Minoso and Chico Carrasquel scored five times apiece.

The 29 runs, 29 hits, and seven home runs are still team records. No AL club has ever scored more runs in a game. Yet just to show how strange baseball can be, the next day the two teams met again on the same field—with almost the same lineups—and the White Sox couldn't get a single runner home. The A's beat Chicago 5–0.

LEGEND HAS IT

WHICH WHITE SOX HITTER HAD THE WORST BATTING SLUMP?

LEGEND HAS IT that Robin Ventura did. In 1990, Ventura won the team's third base job as a rookie. He was hitting over .300 on April 21, and then his bat went silent. Ventura's next hit didn't come until May 11. He was 0–for–41 during that time. This was especially unusual for Ventura. In college, he set a record with a 58-game hitting streak. Luckily, nothing lasts forever. Ventura developed into an excellent hitter. In 1995, he smashed two **grand slams** in one game. Ventura played 10 seasons in Chicago and later returned as the team's manager.

ABOVE: Robin Ventura signed many photos for Chicago fans over the years.   **RIGHT**: Jim Rivera did not think much of the President's penmanship.

Did Jim Rivera refuse a baseball autographed by President John F. Kennedy?

LEGEND HAS IT that he did. On Opening Day in 1961, the White Sox star caught the season's traditional "first pitch" by President Kennedy before a game in Washington, D.C. Rivera asked Kennedy for his autograph on the ball, but he took one look at it and gave it back to the President. "You'll have to do better than that, John," Rivera said. "This is a scribble—I can hardly read it."

Was White Sox ace Mark Buehrle cut from his high school baseball team?

LEGEND HAS IT that he was—not once, but twice! Mark Dunahue, the head coach of Francis Howell North in Missouri, liked the young pitcher. But Dunahue's assistant coaches cut Buehrle in the first two years that he tried out. He finally made the team on his third try. Four years later, Buehrle was pitching in the big leagues for the White Sox. Coach Dunahue now makes all of the final cuts himself—he calls it the "Buehrle Rule."

In 1976, the White Sox were bought by baseball's greatest showman, Bill Veeck. Veeck had owned the team once before, and it had done very well under his leadership. When he returned in 1976, he believed that the White Sox had become boring. Veeck promised fans that he would make Chicago baseball fun again.

One of the first things Veeck did was order different uniforms. When the players and fans saw the new design, they could not believe their eyes. No baseball team had ever worn anything like them. Nothing seemed to match anything else.

The caps spelled out *Sox* in very modern lettering. The uniform tops had no buttons—they were pullover jerseys that were meant to be worn outside the pants, like pajamas. They had v-neck collars with flaps, which looked like a mix of 1870s and 1970s styles. The lettering on these tops did not match the caps—it looked like it was from the turn of the century.

No one knew what to make of the team's new uniform. But Veeck was not finished yet. On hot days, he had his players wear shorts! They may have been cooler than regular baseball pants, but they were no fun

Bill Veeck and five former White Sox unveil Chicago's 1976 uniforms.
Bill Skowron and Moe Drabowsky wear the home whites,
Dave Nicholson and Dan Osinski wear the dark road
styles, and Jim Rivera models the team's famous shorts.

to slide in—ouch! Just as painful were the jokes opponents made about the Chicago players' knobby knees.

Veeck could see how unhappy his players were, so he told them they did not have to wear the shorts anymore. He was disappointed that his experiment failed, but deep down he still believed that his 1976 uniforms were the wave of the future.

TEAM SPIRIT

For 86 years, Chicago baseball fans hoped the White Sox would erase the bad memory of the 1919 World Series. The players who had cheated were punished. All were thrown out of the big leagues. Even so, sometimes White Sox fans felt as if their own "punishment" would never end. Year after year, some bit of bad luck would keep the team from reaching the World Series and winning another championship.

In 2005, the White Sox finally made their championship dreams come true. Their remarkable victory in the World Series set off a joyous celebration in Chicago. Even though the final game was played in Texas, people in Chicago poured into the streets to celebrate. Many had tears in their eyes. When the White Sox returned home, they were given a parade to end all parades. Chicago has never been quite the same again.

LEFT: The White Sox are showered with confetti during the parade to celebrate their 2005 championship.   **ABOVE**: Fans used this window decal during the 1960s.

TIMELINE

Eddie
Collins

1906
The White Sox
win their first
World Series.

1917
Eddie Collins leads
the White Sox to their
second championship.

1901
The team wins the
first AL pennant.

1925
Ted Lyons leads the
AL with 21 wins and
five **shutouts**.

1959
The White Sox win
the AL pennant.

COMISKEY, OWNER OF WHITE SOX

Charles Comiskey
owned the
team from
1901 to 1931.

Luis Aparicio
stole 56 bases
in 1959.

LUIS Aparicio
CHICAGO WHITE SOX S.S.

Jermaine Dye
was named MVP
of the 2005
World Series.

2005
The White Sox win
their third World Series.

2009
Mark Buehrle throws the second
perfect game in team history.

1983
LaMarr Hoyt
wins 24 games.

1994
Frank Thomas wins his
second MVP in a row.

2007
Bobby Jenks retires
41 batters in a row.

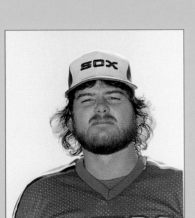

LaMarr
Hoyt

Frank
Thomas

PAT THE BAT

In 1948, Pat Seerey hit four home runs in a game against the Philadelphia A's. The White Sox needed every one—they won 12–11 in extra innings.

RECORD BREAKERS

In 1979, the White Sox asked fans to bring their least favorite disco records to the stadium. They planned to blow them up between games of a doubleheader. So many fans showed up for "Disco Demolition Night" that the crowd could not be controlled, and the White Sox were forced to *forfeit* the second game.

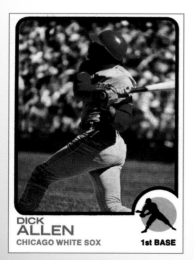

DICK
ALLEN
CHICAGO WHITE SOX   **1st BASE**

FAR AWAY

In the 81 seasons the team played in old Comiskey Park, only seven home runs made it over the distant center field fence. Dick Allen and Richie Zisk were the only Chicago players to hit the ball that far.

TEAM PLAYER

Eddie Collins starred for the White Sox from 1915 to 1926. He also played 13 seasons for the Philadelphia A's. Collins is the only player ever to spend 12 years with two different teams.

ROAD WARRIORS

In 2005, the White Sox won every **postseason** series as the visiting team. No team had ever taken all three on the road.

NEW SOX, OLD SOX

In 1956, 16-year-old Jim Derrington threw a game for the White Sox and became the youngest pitcher in league history. In 1980, the team **activated** their beloved coach, Minnie Minoso. He was 57 at that time. Minoso became the only man ever to play in five different *decades*—the 1940s through the 1980s.

LEFT: Dick Allen shows his power on a 1973 trading card.
ABOVE: Minnie Minoso poses for a photo in 1980.

Bill Veeck

"We can't always guarantee the ball game is going to be good; but we can guarantee the fan will have fun."

▶ **BILL VEECK**, ON SHOWING FANS A GOOD TIME AT THE BALLPARK

"Hitting is more of an attitude than it is a physical approach."

▶ **CARLTON FISK**, ON WHAT MAKES THE BEST HITTERS

"There are no shortcuts to success in baseball."

▶ **FRANK THOMAS**, ON THE VALUE OF HARD WORK

"You don't have to be big to be a big leaguer."

▶ **NELLIE FOX**, *ON THE IMPORTANCE OF SKILL OVER SIZE IN BASEBALL*

"Baseball is the only game that is complicated enough to always be interesting, and yet simple enough to always be understood."

▶ **CHARLES COMISKEY**, *ON WHY BASEBALL IS A GREAT SPORT*

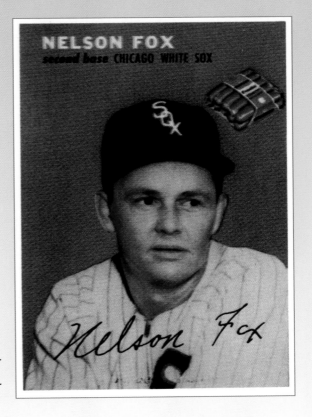

"Never say never in this game because crazy stuff can happen."

▶ **MARK BUEHRLE**, *ON EXPECTING THE UNEXPECTED IN BASEBALL*

"I don't think there is any better feeling than I am feeling right now."

▶ **JOE CREDE**, *AFTER THE WHITE SOX WON THE 2005 WORLD SERIES*

LEFT: Bill Veeck   **ABOVE**: Nelson Fox

39

GREAT DEBATES

People who root for the White Sox love to compare their favorite moments, teams, and players. Some debates have been going on for years! How would you settle these classic baseball arguments?

LUIS APARICIO WAS THE GREATEST WHITE SOX SHORTSTOP EVER ...

... because he won seven **Gold Gloves** and led the AL in stolen bases seven times with Chicago. In the 1950s, the White Sox won with speed and defense. Aparicio was the king of both. He was the Rookie of the Year in 1956 and the team's best player for six years

after that. Aparicio was voted into the Hall of Fame in 1984.

NO WAY! NO ONE WAS MORE AMAZING THAN LUKE APPLING ...

... because 60 years after retiring, he still held the team record for games played and hits. In 1936, Appling (**LEFT**) batted .388. That's a team record, too. Appling played his whole career for the White Sox, 20 seasons in all. He was an All-Star at the age of 40 and hit .301 two seasons later. By the way, Appling is also a Hall of Famer.

FREDDY GARCIA'S VICTORY IN THE 2005 WORLD SERIES WAS THE BEST-PITCHED GAME IN TEAM HISTORY …

… because he threw seven brilliant innings against the Houston Astros to give Chicago the world championship. Garcia faced a lineup full of good hitters. The Astros were playing in their home park. Their **leadoff hitter** reached base in four different innings. Garcia pitched out of trouble each time. The final score was 1–0. Every pitch he threw that night could have made the difference between winning and losing. It was an unforgettable game.

YOU CAN'T GET ANY BETTER THAN MARK BUEHRLE'S NO-HITTER IN 2009 …

… because it was a perfect game. The Tampa Bay Rays sent 27 batters to the plate, and not one made it to first base. Leading off the ninth inning, Gabe Kapler smashed a long fly ball to center field. Dewayne Wise made a great catch. Buehrle

(RIGHT) got the final two outs to pitch the 18th perfect game in big-league history.

FOR THE RECORD

The great White Sox teams and players have left their marks on the record books. These are the "best of the best" …

WHITE SOX AWARD WINNERS

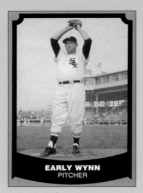

Early Wynn

Frank Thomas

WINNER	AWARD	YEAR
Luis Aparicio	Rookie of the Year	1956
Nellie Fox	Most Valuable Player	1959
Early Wynn	Cy Young Award*	1959
Gary Peters	Rookie of the Year	1963
Tommie Agee	Rookie of the Year	1966
Dick Allen	Most Valuable Player	1972
LaMarr Hoyt	Cy Young Award	1983
Ron Kittle	Rookie of the Year	1983
Tony La Russa	Manager of the Year	1983
Ozzie Guillen	Rookie of the Year	1985
Jeff Torborg	Manager of the Year	1990
Jack McDowell	Cy Young Award	1993
Frank Thomas	Most Valuable Player	1993
Frank Thomas	Most Valuable Player	1994
Jerry Manuel	Manager of the Year	2000
Ozzie Guillen	Manager of the Year	2005
Paul Konerko	ALCS MVP	2005
Jermaine Dye	World Series MVP	2005
Jim Thome	Comeback Player of the Year	2006

The Cy Young Award is given to the league's best pitcher each year.

WHITE SOX ACHIEVEMENTS

ACHIEVEMENT	YEAR
AL Pennant Winner	1901
AL Pennant Winner	1906
World Series Champions	1906
AL Pennant Winner	1917
World Series Champions	1917
AL Pennant Winner	1919
AL Pennant Winner	1959
AL West Champions	1983
AL West Champions	1993
AL Central Champions	1994
AL Central Champions	2000
AL Central Champions	2005
AL Pennant Winner	2005
World Series Champions	2005
AL Central Champions	2008

RAY SCHALK
C.—Chicago White Sox
155

TOP: Ray Schalk was the leader of the 1917 White Sox.
ABOVE: This pin celebrated the team's 1959 pennant.
LEFT: Jim Thome

PINPOINTS

The history of a baseball team is made up of many smaller stories. These stories take place all over the map—not just in the city a team calls "home." Match the pushpins on these maps to the **TEAM FACTS**, and you will begin to see the story of the White Sox unfold!

1 Chicago, Illinois—*The White Sox have played here since 1901.*

2 Detroit, Michigan—*Billy Pierce was born here.*

3 St. Thomas, Pennsylvania—*Nellie Fox was born here.*

4 New York, New York—*The White Sox won the 1917 World Series here.*

Tadahito Iguchi

5 Easton, Maryland—*Harold Baines was born here.*

6 Columbus, Georgia—*Frank Thomas was born here.*

7 Tampa, Florida—*Al Lopez was born here.*

8 Houston, Texas—*The White Sox won the 2005 World Series here.*

9 Los Angeles, California—*The White Sox played in the 1959 World Series here.*

10 Tokyo, Japan—*Tadahito Iguchi was born here.*

11 Ocumare del Tuy, Venezuela—*Ozzie Guillen was born here.*

12 Las Martinas, Cuba—*Jose Contreras was born here.*

GLOSSARY

ACTIVATED—Put a player on the active roster.

AL CENTRAL—A group of American League teams that play in the central part of the country.

AL WEST—A group of American League teams that play in the western part of the country.

ALL-STAR—A player who is selected to play in baseball's annual All-Star Game.

AMERICAN LEAGUE (AL)—One of baseball's two major leagues; the AL began play in 1901.

AMERICAN LEAGUE CHAMPIONSHIP SERIES (ALCS)—The playoff series that has decided the American League pennant since 1969.

CONSISTENT—Doing something again and again at the same level of performance.

DECADES—Periods of 10 years; also specific periods, such as the 1950s.

DRAFT—The annual meeting at which teams take turns choosing the best players in high school and college.

EARNED RUN AVERAGE (ERA)—A statistic that measures how many runs a pitcher gives up for every nine innings he pitches.

FORFEIT—Lose a game because of a rules violation.

GOLD GLOVES—The awards given each year to baseball's best fielders.

GRAND SLAMS—Home runs with the bases loaded.

HALL OF FAME—The museum in Cooperstown, New York, where baseball's greatest players are honored. A player voted into the Hall of Fame is sometimes called a "Hall of Famer."

LEADOFF HITTER—The first hitter in a lineup, or the first hitter in an inning.

MINOR LEAGUES—The many professional leagues that help develop players for the major leagues.

MOST VALUABLE PLAYER (MVP)—The award given each year to each league's top player; an MVP is also selected for the World Series and the All-Star Game.

NATIONAL LEAGUE (NL)—The older of the two major leagues; the NL began play in 1876.

NO-HITTER—A game in which a team does not get a hit.

PENNANT—A league championship. The term comes from the triangular flag awarded to each season's champion, beginning in the 1870s.

PERFECT GAME—A game in which no batter reaches base.

PINSTRIPES—Thin stripes.

PLAYER-MANAGER—A player who also manages his team.

PLAYOFFS—The games played after the regular season to determine which teams will advance to the World Series.

POSTSEASON—The games played after the regular season, including the playoffs and World Series.

PREVAILED—Proved to be more successful or powerful.

ROOKIE OF THE YEAR—The annual award given to each league's best first-year player.

RUNS BATTED IN (RBIs)—A statistic that counts the number of runners a batter drives home.

SHUTOUTS—Games in which one team does not score a run.

TRADITION—A belief or custom that is handed down from generation to generation.

WORLD SERIES—The world championship series played between the AL and NL pennant winners.

EXTRA INNINGS

TEAM SPIRIT introduces a great way to stay up to date with your team! Visit our **EXTRA INNINGS** link and get connected to the latest and greatest updates. **EXTRA INNINGS** serves as a young reader's ticket to an exclusive web page—with more stories, fun facts, team records, and photos of the White Sox. Content is updated during and after each season. The **EXTRA INNINGS** feature also enables readers to send comments and letters to the author! Log onto:

www.norwoodhousepress.com/library.aspx

and click on the tab: **TEAM SPIRIT** to access **EXTRA INNINGS**.

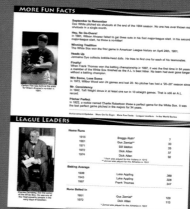

Read all the books in the series to learn more about professional sports. For a complete listing of the baseball, basketball, football, and hockey teams in the **TEAM SPIRIT** series, visit our website at:

www.norwoodhousepress.com/library.aspx

ON THE ROAD

CHICAGO WHITE SOX
333 West 35th Street
Chicago, Illinois 60616
(312) 674-1000
chicago.whitesox.mlb.com

**NATIONAL BASEBALL
HALL OF FAME AND MUSEUM**
25 Main Street
Cooperstown, New York 13326
(888) 425-5633
www.baseballhalloffame.org

ON THE BOOKSHELF

To learn more about the sport of baseball, look for these books at your library or bookstore:

• Augustyn, Adam (editor). *The Britannica Guide to Baseball*. New York, NY: Rosen Publishing, 2011.

• Dreier, David. *Baseball: How It Works*. North Mankato, MN: Capstone Press, 2010.

• Stewart, Mark. *Ultimate 10: Baseball*. New York, NY: Gareth Stevens Publishing, 2009.

PAGE NUMBERS IN BOLD REFER TO ILLUSTRATIONS.

Agee, Tommie 42
Allen, Dick 9, 36, **36**, 42
Altrock, Nick 7
Aparicio, Luis 7, **7**, 21,
25, **34**, 40, 42
Appling, Luke 7, 21, 40, **40**
Baines, Harold 9, **9**, 22, 45
Beckham, Gordon **14**
Buehrle, Mark 10, **11**, 18,
23, 29, 35, 39, 41, **41**
Carrasquel, Chico 27
Cicotte, Eddie 7, 18
Collins, Eddie 7, 18, 34, **34**, 37
Comiskey, Charles 6, 13,
25, **34**, 39
Contreras, Jose 10, 19, 45
Crede, Joe 10, 19, 39
Davis, George 6
Derrington, Jim 37
Drabowsky, Moe **31**
Dunahue, Mark 29
Dye, Jermaine 10, 19, **35**, 42
Faber, Red 7, 18, **18**
Falk, Bibb 7
Felsch, Happy 7
Fernandez, Alex 9
Fisk, Carlton 9, 22, **22**, 38
Fox, Nellie 7, 21, 25,
39, **39**, 42, 45
Garcia, Freddy 10, 19, 41
Garland, Jon 10, 19
Gossage, Goose 9
Griffith, Clark 16
Guillen, Ozzie 10, **10**, 22,
24, 25, 42, 45
Harshman, Jack 27
Horlen, Joel 9
Hoyt, LaMarr **35**, 42
Iguchi, Tadahito 10, 45, **45**
Jackson, Joe 7, 18
Jenks, Bobby 10, 19, 35
John, Tommy 9

Jones, Fielder **6**, 7, 16, 17
Kaat, Jim 9
Kapler, Gabe 41
Kennedy, John F. 29
Kittle, Ron 42
Konerko, Paul **4**, 10, 19, 23, **23**, 42
La Russa, Tony 42
Lollar, Sherm 27, **27**
Lopez, Al 24, **24**, 45
Lyons, Ted 7, 34
Manuel, Jerry 42
McDowell, Jack 9, 42
Melton, Bill 9
Minoso, Minnie 27, 37, **37**
Nicholson, Dave **31**
Nieman, Bob 26, 27
Osinski, Dan **31**
Peters, Gary 9, **15**, 42
Pierce, Billy 7, 21, **21**, 45
Pierzynski, A.J. 10
Podsednik, Scot 10, 19
Rivera, Jim 29, **29**, 31
Robertson, Charlie 23
Rowand, Aaron 19
Schalk, Ray 7, 18, 20, **43**
Seerey, Pat 36
Skowron, Bill **31**
Thomas, Frank **8**, 9, 10, 23,
35, **35**, 38, 42, **42**, 45
Thome, Jim 42, **43**
Torborg, Jeff 42
Uribe, Juan 19
Veeck, Bill 25, 30,
31, **31**, 38, **38**
Ventura, Robin 9, 28, **28**
Walsh, Ed 7, 17, **17**, 20, **20**
Ward, Pete 9
Weaver, Buck 7
Wise, Dewayne 41
Wood, Wilbur 9
Wynn, Early 7, 42, **42**
Zisk, Richie 36

ABOUT THE AUTHOR

MARK STEWART has written more than 50 books on baseball and over 150 sports books for kids. He grew up in New York City during the 1960s rooting for the Yankees and Mets, and was lucky enough to meet players from both teams. Mark comes from a family of writers. His grandfather was Sunday Editor of *The New York Times,* and his mother was Articles Editor of *Ladies' Home Journal* and *McCall's.* Mark has profiled hundreds of athletes over the past 25 years. He has also written several books about his native New York and New Jersey, his home today. Mark is a graduate of Duke University, with a degree in history. He lives and works in a home overlooking Sandy Hook, New Jersey. You can contact Mark through the Norwood House Press website.

ML   3/12